Seven Bridges

Seven Bridges

Jolene Polyack

SEVEN BRIDGES

iUniverse books may be ordered through booksellers or by contacting:

iUniverse
1663 Liberty Drive
Bloomington, IN 47403
www.iuniverse.com
1-800-Authors (1-800-288-4677)

ISBN: 978-1-4917-9182-0 (sc)
ISBN: 978-1-4917-9181-3 (e)

Library of Congress Control Number: 2016904772

Print information available on the last page.

iUniverse rev. date: 04/21/2016

Atlantis

Chapter 1

"Do you think he'll be all right?"

"Of course. The umbilical cord was wrapped around his neck, but I cut it in time. He'll be fine. I am truly heartbroken that I could not save his mother."

"Thank you, Healer. The king will be most grateful to you that at least his heir is alive. I expect you'll be rewarded handsomely. Oh, look! His little eyes are open! What a beautiful little man he is!"

"That he is. I hope he will be a great king one day, too. Atlantis needs a strong hand to guide and lead her. I will be in my chambers if you need anything. Good night, Amayah."

As the healer retired to his room, Amayah's concerned expression transformed into a cold and calculating smirk. She would be the nursemaid to the new prince. Years of planning and positioning had placed her here, in the palace of the great king and queen of Atlantis, at this very moment. She hung a purple handkerchief from the window, indicating to the handful of coconspirators below that Atlantis had a new prince and all was well.

Chapter 2

"Eight, nine, ten. *Amayah!* I'm coming!"

Prince Kewab searched the palace for his nursemaid. She was his best friend, and he loved her very much. She indulged him nearly anything, unless it put his life in danger. No other person save his father, the king, had more influence on the young prince than Amayah.

"*There* you are!" Prince Kewab screeched with excitement. His dimples exaggerated as he did so. "I knew you would hide in the kitchen. You always do." His voice was filled with laughter and adoration. She could do nothing wrong in his eyes.

"My prince." Amayah bowed deeply. "You are so clever! Where can I hide where you cannot find me?" she asked rhetorically. She hugged the prince and rocked him back and forth gently.

"This does not look like education!" boomed the voice of the king, his entire face turning bright red with anger. He had been standing at the doorway watching the two secretly. "This is not how I instructed you to prepare the prince for ruling this land one day. If you cannot adhere to my wishes, I'll find someone who will. There will not be another opportunity for you to ignore my commands!" The king turned and walked away regally, with several servants following closely.

"Amayah, I'm sorry," said the prince in a hushed voice. "It's my fault, I know. I promise to be a better student and not get the king mad at you again."

"Shhhh, little one. It is my fault. I cannot deny you anything. But we both must be more careful if I am to stay with you," Amayah said as she looked out of the nearby window, noticing a purple handkerchief in the distance among the trees. She took his hand and led him back to his section of the palace.

"Here, Kewab. Start working on your diagram of the kingdom. You must learn every element that makes Atlantis work. Your father will be looking to review this soon, so make it perfect. I'm going to go for a walk while you concentrate." She bowed to the prince and walked out of his rooms, through the long corridors, out to the courtyard and into the forest where the handkerchief had been waving.

Chapter 3

Amayah walked up to Ba'ale and hugged him tightly. The two began to kiss, softly at first and then with passion and forcefulness. At last, Ba'ale said, "Every time I see you, you are more beautiful than the last." He stroked her hair back away from her face and peered into her emerald green eyes.

Amayah ran her finger along his cleft chin as she peered back into Ba'ale's eyes and smiled seductively. She felt little for him, just as she felt little for the prince. She was growing tired and bored of the charade she had been playing for so long.

When she had agreed to position herself as the nursemaid of the new prince, it had sounded fun and exciting. Yet she didn't like children, didn't like the stuffiness of the palace, and didn't like orders being barked at her. Unfortunately, it was too late to back out now. The plan was in full swing, and the end was in sight.

"Kewab is easily manipulated. He loves me and will do anything I ask. He will reach puberty soon, and we can begin the next phase," Amayah said softly in Ba'ale's ear, nibbling his lobe as she spoke. If anyone was spying on them, it would look like a lover's rendezvous instead of a strategic meeting to control Atlantis's governing family.

Ba'ale responded by kissing her throat and pulling her closer. He believed that he would be ruling by Amayah's side in the future and that he would be able to have her whenever he wanted. The group's plan had proceeded for years without a hitch. The closer they got to the prize, the more anticipatory each became. He whispered, "The potions will be ready when you are, my love, as will I." He buried his face into her hair and deeply inhaled her scent. It would have to be enough of her to last until their next meeting.

Amayah waited in the forest until Ba'ale was long gone. She collected the little white flowers that grew in the rays of sunlight that broke through the treetops and touched the earth. She used this quiet time to mentally review both the conspirator's plan and her own personal one. The two plans currently converged; however, the time was nearing when these two paths would part ways. Amayah would need to be very careful—otherwise, she would be very dead.

Chapter 4

Prince Kewab was a good boy. He had led a life of privilege, knowing and understanding that he would one day take his father's place on the throne as king of Atlantis. His father had been preparing him for that day almost since his birth. However, as prepared as the young prince was on an educational level, he was emotionally far less ready to run a country.

One day, while playing in the royal garden, he spied Amayah heading for the forest. He decided to secretly follow her. He kept her in sight, but far enough away that she would not hear his footsteps on the forest floor. Much to his shock and ire, Amayah started running right into the arms of a man. The prince's blood ran cold. He was furious. He marched in full view up to the couple and sharply pulled on Amayah's arm.

"What do you think you are doing?" the prince demanded.

The man immediately released Amayah. Both of them looked terrified and pale.

"This is my brother, Ba'ale. I didn't know he was here and am delighted to see him," Amayah said shakily.

"Do you think I'm *stupid?* That is not how one hugs one's brother, Amayah!" the prince said incredulously. Fire was shooting out of his eyes as he glared first at Amayah and then at Ba'ale.

"I think I should leave now, my lady—Prince," Ba'ale bowed to both and swiftly departed into the woods.

Amayah ran to Kewab and tried to hug him. He pushed her away and turned his back to her as he folded his arms. Amayah gently caressed his shoulders; he did not stop her.

She began stroking his neck as she stepped closer, placing the other hand on his arm and moving it up and down his biceps.

"My prince," she whispered in his ear. "I am so sorry that I've offended you. I think it is time we were honest with each other about our feelings."

Kewab turned slowly so that he was inches away from her face. He had grown as tall as she was now, and his voice was beginning to change. He had a few hairs peeking out from his chin and the side of his face. He shuddered at the feeling he got being so unexpectedly close to her in this manner.

"Do you love him?" he asked with a hurt voice.

"Of course not. I told you, he's my brother. Please don't be jealous, Kewab. There is only one man for me."

Jealous? The prince had never felt jealousy before. There had never been anything to be jealous of. He stood back and mentally digested the accusation. Amayah stood motionless. After several moments, the prince looked into Amayah's eyes and asked almost imperceptibly, "Who is the only man for you, Amayah?"

"Who do you think it is, Kewab?" she said, slightly seductively. A thin smile slowly stretched across her face.

The prince swallowed hard, his Adam's apple noticeably moving down and then up again. His eyes widened as he stepped closer to Amayah, not knowing what to do next. Amayah read his indecisiveness and reached for his hands, placing them on either side of her face. She placed her hands on his face and began to draw him closer until their lips touched.

"I've seen quite enough," the king roared as he swiftly approached the couple. He had followed Kewab at some distance. "Amayah, gather your belongings and leave the palace immediately. How dare you behave this way to my son, the prince of Atlantis! You are lucky I do not have you beheaded for this. Now leave at once!"

Amayah looked at Kewab with tears in her eyes. She looked at the king and bowed, then turned and ran as fast as she could to the palace.

The prince was terrified. There was so much to process; he was overwhelmed. He stood paralyzed, waiting for instructions from his father.

The king ordered his men to escort his son back to the palace and to not leave his side. "I will deal with you later, in private," he said over his shoulder as he briskly strode back to the palace.

Chapter 5

Amayah made her way back to her room and began packing her things. It was a little early to begin implementing her plan, but now she had no choice. There had always been contingencies for unexpected situations, and she felt no remorse for putting herself in this position now. She took a small pouch out of the inner side compartment of her bag and concealed it in one hand. With the other, she lifted the bag containing all of her possessions and placed the strap on her shoulder. She looked slowly around her room and allowed a brief smile to cross her face. Then, she closed the door and headed for the kitchen.

***

That evening, as the king ate his dinner, his throat began to contract. Just a little at first, but then more and more until he could not breathe. He panicked, jumping up from his fine hand-carved wooden chair, clasping his throat with one hand and wildly waving the other. His servants rushed toward him, attempting to discern what was happening and how they might help him. His eyes rolled up into their sockets, and his body went limp. The king of Atlantis was dead, suddenly and unexpectedly.

***

Kewab was in his chambers when one of the servants ran in to tell him the news. The blood drained from his face, and his heart began to pound. Anger and frustration were replaced with shock and fear. He would become King of Atlantis now. He had never looked forward to the title; in fact it had always sounded so intimidating that he seldom thought about it. When others mentioned it, he quickly changed the subject.

As terrible and insensitive as he knew it would sound, he asked the servant anyway: "Find Amayah and bring her to me at once." The servant bowed stoically and turned to do the new king's bidding. Kewab dressed and proceeded to the main hall. The palace was in full chaos, and he did not know what to do to bring peace to the situation. It occurred to him that if it were out of control here, it would certainly be that way in all of Atlantis soon. The kingdom would be in jeopardy if he didn't restore a ruling hand. He approached the throne and stopped, unsure if he should sit there or not. Such protocol had never been discussed. His father had taught him many things but had not yet prepared a succession plan.

"My king," he heard the familiar and welcomed voice of Amayah approaching. He turned and looked at her pleadingly. She slightly nodded toward the throne. Kewab understood what she meant.

He sat in his father's—no, his—ornate oversized throne and assessed the people gathering in the great hall. The sound of many hushed conversations resonated off the stone walls. Amayah bowed deeply and asked to approach the king. He held out his hand and slowly curled his fingers up, indicating that she may. She knelt at his feet and looked into his eyes.

"You've been trained all of your life to be King of Atlantis. You will make a most excellent ruler, my king. You are ready," Amayah whispered assuredly.

Kewab looked out at the large crowd now gathered in the hall and pronounced, "Today is a dark day for Atlantis. Today the most successful and respected king in all of history has died. We will mourn his death and bury him appropriately."

His father's spiritual advisor walked to the side of the throne and announced, "All hail King Kewab. Long live the king!" The crowd roared in unison, restating the pronouncement repeatedly until Kewab motioned for them to stop.

Later, Kewab and Amayah were in his chambers having a small meal. The events of the day had been too much for the new king, and he needed to recover privately. Already many people were clamoring to be in his inner circle, or wanted his ear on a subject that they felt needed immediate attention. He was overwhelmed and in mourning. He just wanted to be left alone with Amayah.

"There will be much work to be done, my king," she said as they both picked at the food on their golden plates. "Would you have me stay to help?"

"Amayah, I can't do this. I can't do any of this. But if I don't, Atlantis will fall." He dropped his fork, placed both hands over his eyes, and began to cry.

"Shhh, Kewab. You can do this. You will do this. I will help you. Everyone will help you. You're ready, my king." Amayah had moved next to him, standing above him and stroking his hair. He looked up at her and slowly stood so that they were face-to-face. She brushed the tears from his cheeks then kissed each side. Kewab responded by kissing both of her cheeks. She moved her lips to his and tentatively kissed him. He responded by kissing her slightly harder. Just then there was a knock at the door. Kewab flinched, not only because the knock was unexpected, but because just hours before, if it had been his father, there would have been another scene. The realization hit Kewab that he could now be with Amayah as much as he wanted without retribution. He took one step away from her, grabbed her hand, and said, "Enter."

When the servant had left, he turned back to Amayah, holding her hands with both of his and asked, "Will you be my queen?"

"No, Kewab. I will not," Amayah responded decisively.

"But why? Every king has a queen, and I need you. I can't do this alone. We both know that. I can't imagine another person I trust more than you," Kewab pleaded.

"All you speak of is needing me—nothing about loving me. Kewab, a husband and wife should love each other, even a king and queen. Besides, I'm too old for you. I raised you. People will think it's strange."

"You know I've loved you my entire life. Maybe not the same way I do now, but I've always loved you. You are not too old. You were just a child, practically, yourself when they brought you here to be my nursemaid. I don't care what anyone says. I can't imagine anyone else."

"Then I should leave. Perhaps with me gone, you will be able to more easily find someone suitable to rule with you," Amayah said sadly.

"No!" Kewab slammed his fist on the table, causing the plates and goblets to rattle. "Please, Amayah, *please.* Be my queen." He knelt on one leg, taking her hand and kissing it. "I do need you, but I also love you now and forever. Do not make me suffer more on a day like today by denying me your hand in marriage." He looked up at her pleadingly.

Amayah looked down at the new king. She knelt down in front of him and whispered softly, "Yes."

Chapter 6

Cloaked in a hooded garment that hid her face, Amayah stole into the nearby village. She quietly knocked on one of the doors lining the main street after looking around to confirm that no one had seen her. Once the door opened, she stepped into the meager home and closed the door. She was led down a long corridor, passing rudimentary furniture and fixtures. At the end of the corridor was another room, which she entered without hesitation. This room sharply contrasted the others. Here the walls were filled with ornate tapestries and golden paint. A large, embellished round table sat in the middle of the room with heavy, tall-backed chairs placed around it. Amayah sat at the table, joining the others.

As she sat, a steady stream of servants began bringing in platter after platter of lavish food and carafes of fine wine. The clanging of silver cutlery against silver platters resonated off the walls. Laughter mingled with the sound of wine being poured into beautiful goblets around the table. As plates and goblets were filled, the room was momentarily quieted.

"To Amayah!" A man dressed in the golden cloak said as he raised his silver goblet.

"To Amayah!" everyone in the room responded joyously.

"To Amayah," whispered Ba'ale in Amayah's ear. "My queen."

Amayah laughed and raised her glass to the jovial group. "Thank you for choosing me to help carry out your plan. It has been too long since the rightful heirs to the throne were humiliated and tricked out of the palace. It will bring me great pleasure to see you at your rightful place again!"

Raucous, celebratory sounds began to once again fill the room. The carafes were refilled as the guests continued their festivities. As the night wore on, conversation shifted to the specifics of the final part of their plan. After the official coronation of Kewab and the consummation of his marriage to Amayah, Kewab would meet with an untimely and tragic accident, leaving Amayah the sole ruler of Atlantis. After an appropriate time of mourning, she would then court and marry Ba'ale. Once again, the Vicinus family would be in control of Atlantis.

Amayah had no intention of ruling alongside anyone. She would have to make her move now, while the entire Vicinus family was here together and filled with wine.

In her pocket were pouches of the same substance with which she had laced Kewab's father's food. This time it would be more difficult, with so many people needing to ingest the poison at once. If even one person lived, she would have a much larger problem on her hands. Amayah stood and reached for one of the carafes of wine. She secretly poured the contents of one of the vials into the carafe and began pouring wine into the goblets of each guest. As she did this, she asked each person to wait so that she might give a toast herself to the new ruling family. By the time she finished, each goblet, including hers, was filled with the tainted wine.

She raised her goblet and said, "At last, the Vicinus family will be in power again. At last, Ba'ale will be not only *my* king, but King of Atlantis. At last, we will all get what we desire and deserve! All hail King Ba'ale!" She aimed her goblet to Ba'ale and pretended to drink. Each family member hailed the new king and drank.

Amayah excused herself from the great room, pretending the need to relieve herself. She continued through the long hallway and left quickly out the front door, walking briskly back to the palace.

Chapter 7

Kewab's coronation was extravagant. Amayah had overseen the entire event and created a celebration like none that had come before. She seldom left his side and controlled much of what went on around the couple. She had explained to Kewab that Atlantis needed to see him and know that the country was in strong hands. She insisted on a grand tour in order for all of the subjects to believe in his ability to rule. Of course, with her by his side, Amayah would also be associated with ruling, and it would make it easier for her to take over once Kewab was disposed of.

The month-long tour also gave Amayah more insight into the infrastructure and workings of the country. Their advanced public works system and technology were unique to Atlantis. No other country had such resources, and as a result whoever ruled Atlantis controlled the rest of the world. It was as if the country had been placed and populated in this world from somewhere else and that the indigenous people were far less intelligent. Atlantians and those who visited that country all sensed the superiority, yet could not fully understand how or why it was so.

When they returned from the tour, Amayah began preparation for their royal wedding. It would be far less extravagant than the coronation. She did not think Kewab would be able to handle much more fanfare, and she wanted to hurry along with her plan. The sooner she became queen, the sooner she could remove Kewab from her life and finally do as she pleased, when she pleased.

Their wedding was set in a nearby temple, with only a few invited to witness the event. Amayah wanted a simple wedding so that people would not think she was marrying

Kewab for his money or power. She wanted it to appear that the two were truly in love and that nothing else mattered. For the most part, no one suspected otherwise. Amayah had been in Kewab's life from the beginning and had done an excellent job of pretending to love and adore him. It had only seemed natural for the two to be together now, despite their difference in age.

As the ceremony concluded, the ground quaked unexpectedly. The sudden force was shocking. It felt as if the entire country were on a ship in a stormy ocean as the ground rocked back and forth.

Chapter 8

The king and queen of Atlantis had been ruling for months. It was clear that Amayah was more suited for the position than the true heir. Kewab remained immature and incapable of being serious for long stretches of time. There was concern over the frequency and severity of earthquakes, which had begun plaguing the land on their wedding day.

Amayah had studied the country's infrastructure enough to know and understand the importance of keeping the roads, sewer, water, and power supplies intact. She had shifted the military's efforts to maintaining these essential services and less on protecting the kingdom from potential intruders.

Ba'ale and his family were successfully wiped out, thanks to their own potion. Amayah had held onto pouches of the substance until it was time to do away with Kewab. He had impregnated her, and she would soon be giving birth to a daughter. Only the healers of Atlantis could tell the gender of the unborn—yet another example that set them apart from the rest of the world.

Chapter 9

"Breathe, Amayah. Breathe!"

"I *am* breathing, you idiot!" Amayah growled through her teeth at the healer. She was covered in sweat, her hair wet and sticking to her face. Outside, Kewab waited with great concern. He had never been ready to rule, and he certainly wasn't ready to be a father. The thought made him nauseous. But most of all, he was nervous for the health and wellbeing of his beautiful wife. His mother had died in childbirth. He couldn't bear life if he lost Amayah now.

Suddenly, a burst of crying filled the hallway. His daughter had been born. No one with such lungs would be unhealthy, he thought. When he heard Amayah laugh, he immediately ran into the chamber to see for himself. The smile on his face quickly melted away when he saw Amayah. He knelt beside her and carefully took her hand. "Are you all right?" he asked gently.

"I just had my insides ripped out, King. So, no, I am not all right at the moment. But I am healthy, if that is what you mean," she snapped at him.

"I am sorry to insult you, Queen. But you look so distressed. I was afraid."

"Your words are doing nothing to comfort me," she snapped again. Kewab irritated her with his slowness, and she was in no mood to act differently than she felt at this moment. "Please, Kewab, I would like privacy now," she said as she turned her back away from him.

The healer handed the newborn, swaddled in a blanket, to Kewab. Kewab looked at the infant, startled. It was red and wrinkly and didn't look like a small person at all. It occurred to him that he had never seen a newborn baby before. Remembering that Amayah wanted to be alone, he carried the baby out of the chambers and into the throne room. He would show his subjects the newest member of the ruling family. As he sat down on his throne, the ground shook violently. He had to hold onto the chair with one arm while clutching the baby with the other.

Chapter 10

Septima grew and grew and before long began walking. She was a delight to the king and queen. Amayah had delayed killing Kewab because he had become so engrossed with Septima that he left her alone to rule the kingdom. She thought it ironic that she had raised him, and now he was raising their daughter. Since Kewab's maturity was closer to Septima's than her own, he spent countless hours with their child, and Amayah was enjoying far more privacy than she had in a very long time. The urgency to rule alone had waned with the king's attention focused elsewhere.

While Amaya was hearing the daily updates regarding the rapidly dilapidating plumbing system, the throne room was filled with a cry that caused everyone's blood to run cold. It was the most horrific sound anyone had ever heard. Then, "Amayah! Amayah! Amayah!" came the shriek of Kewab's nearly unintelligible voice coming from the hallway.

"What is it?" Amayah demanded, surprised at the urgency in his voice. As he stepped out of the hall and into view, there were gasps from throughout the room. Kewab was carrying the limp body of Septima in his arms. He had begun to hyperventilate and could speak no more.

Amayah ran toward them and looked first at her daughter's limp body and then at her face. Realization struck her almost immediately. The facial coloring—it was the same as Kewab's father when she had laced his food with the potion. Hoping she was wrong, she raced toward her chamber and to her hiding place where she had kept the potion all this time. The pillow that had housed the potion secretly in its innards had been opened, and the pouch lay on the ground, open and empty. Amayah dropped to her knees and began to weep. Of all the people she had destroyed to get to the place she was today, she would undo everything just to bring her little girl back to life. She would give up ruling and the luxury of the palace just to have her back. Horror, shame, and guilt washed over her in wave upon wave until it was unbearable. Amayah curled up on the floor next to the pouch and could do nothing.

The ground began to revolt more violently than ever before. It felt as if the land had risen several feet and then come crashing down. It kept doing this over and over. Then, the earth opened up and swallowed everything.

Bridge

"Why am I here?"

"Why do you think you are here? What do you remember?"

"I was in Atlantis with Septima in my arms. She was dead. The ground began to give way, and now I'm here. It's all white. I cannot see or feel. I have no body! I only have my thoughts! Am I dead? Is this death?"

"There is no death. Only enlightenment. You are very new. You will stay here and consider what you experienced in Atlantis. When you are ready, you will learn more."

"When will I be ready?"

"That is for you to decide. You will know, and then you will begin another lesson."

"How will I know?"

Egypt

Chapter 11

Amam and Khaba played with sticks in the road. Their bare feet were covered in desert dust. With less than a year separating the two, they almost looked like twins. They behaved that way too, each knowing what the other was thinking before it was said.

They were part of a large family who farmed wheat on the outskirts of Cairo along the Nile. There was not usually much time for play, but today most of the family had traveled into Cairo to sell their crop at the local bazaar. The boys were too young to go, and, quite frankly, the family preferred to keep them at home since they required more supervision than anything else.

Amam's emerald green eyes peered out from his long, dark, unkempt hair toward his brother.

"Let's go swimming," he said with a grin.

The family being gone was like a holiday for the two brothers. When their family left them like this, once each year, they did whatever they could imagine to take advantage of the freedom. Farmer's work was long, hard, and never-ending. They had to pack an entire year's worth of child's play into this one day. They raced from one activity to another. Nearly all of their adventures would have garnered whippings if they had ever been caught.

Khaba immediately pulled his shirt off and flung it to the ground. He raced to the river, intending on beating his brother to the edge. Amam's heavy breathing grew closer behind him; he might overtake him soon. The two made it to the bank at nearly the exact same time. Neither stopped. Both flung their bodies into the cool water without hesitation or abandon.

It wasn't long before they became bored. After all, there were so many other things to do before their family returned. They couldn't spend too much time on just one activity. Khaba suggested, "Let's go to the silo!" They grabbed their clothes and headed toward the tall cylindrical structure near the dirt road of their property. Both climbed up the sides like lizards until they reached the top. Clearly this wasn't their first time.

"Let's jump in!" said Khaba with a long smile bookmarked by dimples.

"How will we get out?" retorted Amam.

"Through the door at the bottom. It'll be unlocked, since they just emptied most of the wheat out."

"What if it's not unlocked?"

"Then we'll climb back up!" Khaba said, the octave of his voice ascending on the last word. As he said it, he jumped into the silo. On his way down, his foot somehow caught on one of the side rungs. His body jerked from the fall, and he heard a loud *snap*. His leg was not equipped to take the sudden halt of motion. Excruciating pain pulsed through his body, and he released a guttural scream. His shaking hands reached for the rung to try to lift his foot out of the predicament, but shock had rendered him unable to do so. He looked down and realized that if he did release his foot, he would land on his head or back. Neither seemed like a good idea.

Amam had watched with fear as his brother had been caught. He called down to him, "I don't know what to do. What do you want me to do?"

"I don't know! I don't know! It hurts! I can't get my foot free, and if I do, I'll fall backward!" Panic gripped both boys.

"Let me think!" Amam yelled down.

"Hurry! I think I'm going to pass out, Amam. Hurry!" Khaba's voice was getting weak and jittery. He began to shiver from the shock.

Amam climbed down the inside of the silo until he reached his brother. "Can you put your arms around my neck?" he asked.

Khaba shook his head. "I don't think so. You're too far up. I can't bend that much."

"You'll have to. I can't think of anything else to do. On the count of three, thrust yourself toward my neck, and I'll get as low as I can so you can wrap your arms around me. Please, I can't think of anything else.

"One …

"Two …

"Three."

As the brothers attempted to meet midair, Khaba was able to grab onto Amam's neck, but the momentum was too much for Amam to hold himself on the rung and take on the added weight of his brother. Amam fell to the bottom of the silo and hit the minute amount of remaining wheat with a thud. The shift in his own weight allowed Khaba's foot to free itself from its own rung, and he fell down, landing on his brother. Both boys remained motionless.

Chapter 12

When the family returned home, they could not find the brothers anywhere. They were aware of the boys' annual "celebration" when left alone on the farm; the family thought it better that they didn't know exactly what the boys did while they were away. However, there was no sign of them anywhere now. Curiosity was replaced with worry and then panic when no one could find the two. They looked into the night with torches, not wanting to leave them out in the dark. At last, their mother heard moans coming from the silo and discovered two very badly injured boys lying on the small pile of wheat. If they weren't so injured, they would have been beaten for taking such a risk.

Stretchers were quickly built to carry the boys to the house. Each was placed carefully in their own bed. Amam recovered fully, but Khaba was unable to move from his neck down.

Once it was clear that Khaba would never walk again, the family took turns taking care of him. It was difficult to be on a farm with not only one less worker, but also the added burden of taking care of someone who could do nothing for himself.

Amam was haunted with guilt. He felt partially responsible for his brother's injury. He was Khaba's primary caregiver. In a strange way, they became closer as a result of the accident. As the two grew into young men, it became apparent that the situation could not continue as it was. Khaba had found a way to be useful to the family by thinking of unique solutions to challenges in farming, or in life for that matter. The endless hours lying motionless provided him with the time to exercise his mind exclusively. He became the person family members would come to for advice. As word spread, friends and neighbors would also come to receive answers to life's problems from a man who could not move.

He had encouraged his brother Amam to leave the family farm and find his own way. Amam had at first refused to leave his brother's side. However, as Khaba's reputation grew as a problem-solver and more and more people came to him for answers, Amam felt less and less needed. He eventually left the farm and made the long trek to Cairo to see what the city might have to offer.

When at last he returned home, he brought his new wife, Bataanta, to meet the family. Everyone was thrilled at the new union and began preparation for a large feast to celebrate. As the women cooked, Amam took the time to talk to his brother privately.

"How are you feeling, my brother?" he asked after a long and heartfelt hug.

"I am very well, Amam. It is so good to see you. How was Cairo?"

"Cairo is amazing. I wish you could have come with me. I was very lonely at first, but once I met Bataanta everything changed. She is from the city and helped me to make a life for myself there. Do you approve of my new wife, brother?" Amam asked, somewhat rhetorically.

"I love you more than anything, Amam. You know that. But from the moment I met Bataanta, my blood turned cold. I cannot explain it," Khaba responded pensively.

"That is similar to what she said upon meeting you. You are the two people I love the most in this world, yet you do not approve of each other. Jealousy, do you think?"

"No, not jealousy. I wish for you to have a wife and be happy. I do not know what makes my mind respond the way it does to her. I am concerned, though. Please be careful with her, Amam."

Amam laughed, kissed his brother on the top of his head, and left to help prepare for the feast.

Chapter 13

Bataanta and Amam returned to Cairo and continued to live their lives there. Khaba remained on the family farm and assisted with advice and wisdom whenever it was needed. When the couple's first child was old enough to travel, they returned to the family farm to introduce their new addition to everyone.

Amam brought the toddler to Khaba.

"I would like for you to meet Janais. Janais, this is your Uncle Khaba."

Khaba smiled at the young boy and said, "I am honored to meet you, Janais. You look just like your father, and strong too."

The boy's face turned bright red. All he could do was to bow and say, "Thank you, Uncle."

Standing at the doorway was Bataanta. As she watched her son and Khaba, her lips pursed, making her cleft chin more noticeable.

Amam said, "We are moving back to the farm, Khaba. Cairo is no place to raise a child. We want Janais to grow up on a farm, and Father has indicated that he could use my help."

"This is excellent news, Amam! I look forward to seeing you and your family every day. I've missed you, and it will be pleasurable to enjoy your company and get to know your fine son!"

Chapter 14

Amam struggled on the farm. He had lived in Cairo for so long that he was out of shape. It took him twice as much effort to do the work that he had done easily as a boy. He began to remember how difficult and unending farming was and became remorseful that he had moved his family back here.

The nights were unsettlingly quiet. There was nothing to do but work. He became resentful of Khaba, who was able to sit in the house all day, being waited on for every little need and having people come from far and wide to talk to him. It was only now that he was back and working hard in the fields that he began to feel this way. He was angry with himself not only for moving back, but also for feeling this unexpected anger toward his brother. Had it been there all along, lying dormant? Or was it only manifesting now? Amam did not know.

One evening as the family sat down for dinner, Janais insisted on sitting next to his uncle. The two had become extremely close and clearly took delight in each other's company. Amam slammed his hand on the table and bellowed, "You will sit here next to me, Janais, and you will do so now!"

The room became silent as everyone stared at Amam in shock. He had been careful to conceal his feelings of jealousy but had now revealed them so plainly that even little Janais knew how he felt.

The next morning, Amam, Bataanta, and Janais loaded their cart to return to Cairo. Amam felt ashamed and understood that there would be no recovery from his outburst the night before. He had always seen himself as the favored son and now knew, without doubt, that he was in fact the fallen one. He could not bear to look at his family anymore.

Once their possessions were packed, Amam hugged his mother, father, and siblings. He had no intention of returning. His father asked him to go in and say goodbye to Khaba. Amam refused. He did not want to see his brother again. As he turned to climb into the cart, Janais bolted for the house and into Khaba's room. He ran to his uncle and hugged him tightly, tears streaming down his bright red face.

"I do not want to go, Uncle! I want to stay here with you! Please. Talk my father into letting me stay here!"

Khaba shook his head slowly, sadness in his eyes. "No, my nephew. You must go with your family. I will always be here for you once you've come of age, but for now, you must be with your parents. I love you, Janais, and your father too. Be sure to tell him that. You are all welcome back here whenever you choose.

As they pulled out of the dirt path and onto the main road that would take them to Cairo, Bataanta became more animated and jovial. She had not liked farm living at all and was delighted that her husband had decided to return to the liveliness of the city. She would see to it that they never returned.

Khaba died a few months later. He had exceeded the life expectancy for a person with his condition and knew that when Amam and his family left, he would not see any of them again. His mother thought he died of a broken heart, for Khaba loved his brother and nephew immensely. Khaba would probably have agreed if the topic had ever been discussed prior to his passing.

Bridge

"Ah, it is nice to be back here. I had forgotten how peaceful it is."

"Yes. It is time for you to discover what lessons you've added to your education."

"I wonder—why was not Septima with me this time? I loved her so much in Atlantis."

"She was with you; you just did not recognize her. Is there anything you wish to discuss?"

"Yes. Why does Amayah hate me so?"

"Hate? Is that what you think it is?"

"Of course. I see now that she has never loved me, even though I'd always thought that she did."

"There is no hate. There is only learning and growing intellectually. Emotions are something that the young have not yet learned to identify—they are how you feel about others in relation and comparison to yourself. This is a very adolescent thing, and you will eventually shed these burdens. Now ponder what you have learned so that you may have another lesson."

Rome

Chapter 15

"Today you will each begin to become men," bellowed General Scipio. "None of you have the slightest idea what that means, but you will. When the Roman Army has finished training each of you, you will have no fear. You will have no uncertainty. You will have a strong body and mind. You will be decisive and fearless."

He gave this same speech to each group of new Roman soldiers. It was meant to set the stage for what would be a difficult and grueling introduction to life as a soldier. Most of the men who decided to join the Roman army were poor and had few other options. Most were young and hopeful that this would be the career for them.

The men trained mercilessly for four months, walking miles each day and each carrying over thirty pounds of equipment and supplies. The life was difficult, but there was great pride in being a part of the Roman Army. Never had the world seen such power and discipline. Men joined for various reasons with the understanding that they would be in for twenty-five years. Upon retirement, they would be given a small parcel of land and a pension for their service. This was something that many of the families would not have otherwise.

Kornelius had joined because he looked forward to the singular purpose and physical discipline that the army would provide him. He wanted the brotherhood of a unit, and quite frankly, he had little prospects for a career back home in Milan, where he was one of many children being raised by a single mother who was seldom home.

Toward the end of their months of training, the men in his unit were huddled beneath their goatskin tent. It was a cold night, and they had worked extraordinarily hard that day. As they unrolled their bedding, Britannicus broke into song. None of the other men were in any mood for such merriment in the midst of such exhaustion.

"Britannicus, must you be so consistent in your ability to choose the most inappropriate time to demonstrate your lack of vocal talent?" Kornelius said, his dimples more noticeable due to the straight line his lips were making across his face.

"Why, Kornelius, as usual you're merely demonstrating your jealousy of both my timing and my talent. But alas, I do forgive you and understand that you must be feeling quite tired after today's work," Britannicus retorted in a light and taunting way.

"Must you two quarrel each and every day?" Atticus said, reproaching them. "Can we have a quiet evening, just this once? Surely you can both get along for a mere few hours." As he said this, he lay down on his back, closed his emerald green eyes, and lifted his hands to cradle the back of his head. Within seconds, he was snoring steadily. Before long, the remainder of the unit joined Atticus in slumber. The Roman Army did not leave excessive energy untapped by the end of each day.

The following morning, the unit was deployed toward the north to aid in fighting the Celts. Their training was over. As General Scipio had promised, the men had been transformed from commoners to strong, disciplined fighting machines. While they continued to banter and joke with each other, as they progressed in their careers their individual interactions became fewer and fewer. In the Roman Army there was only one goal and only one focus. Emotion was not encouraged or welcome within the ranks.

The journey north was arduous. Kornelius' unit was one of ten within a century of men. They walked many miles each day, lugging several pounds of necessities on their bodies. Each night they would make a new camp, structured in the exact same way, digging trenches and erecting a protective wooden fence around the perimeter called a palisade. Despite the grueling march of the day, each man took turns on watch at night.

Kornelius rose in the middle of the night to relieve Julius on the second week of their journey north. To his dismay, he discovered Julius sleeping at the edge of the palisade. He withdrew his *gladius* and nudged Julius to awaken him. Julius, startled, jumped up and drew his own sword toward Kornelius.

"You were asleep!" hissed Kornelius. "The punishment is death if anyone finds out. You know that."

"I am not well. I should not have been on watch tonight." Julius whispered, his bright red face shimmering in the moonlight along with the moisture in his eyes.

Kornelius had always liked Julius, but he also held him in a sort of reverence. He did not know exactly why; it was just a feeling. Maybe it was the way Julius talked or held himself. But for whatever reason, he was disappointed that Julius had committed such an unforgivable crime. He was loyal to his brother-in-arms, but he was more loyal to his general and to the Roman Empire. He turned and strode to the centurion's tent to report Julius.

The next morning, after camp was packed away, the remaining men of the unit were called to the front of the century. Julius was held by two guards. The pronouncement was made that he had been found sleeping while on watch. Atticus and Britannicus were selected to escort him to the edge of the nearby cliff. As they walked, there was complete silence within the ranks. Killing men who did not obey orders was relatively common and meant to remind the soldiers that there was no tolerance for disobedience. As they reached the edge, there was no hesitation to push Julius off the cliff. He did not protest or make a sound as his body fell to meet the jagged rocks below. The sound resonated up to the century, and with it the command to fall into rank and begin marching. There would be no mourning, no pleasantries about Julius, and no pension to his family. His family would receive a letter stating that he had betrayed the Roman Army and shame would prevail around the family for years to come.

Chapter 16

Left, right, left, right, left, right. The monotony of endless marching lulled Kornelius into a state of oblivion. Each day began, unfolded, and ended the same way. At first he thought about Julius and his decision to turn him in. Then his thoughts wandered to the future and what it might be like to be retired from the military and farming a small piece of land in the country. Once he ran out of things to think about and there was little time for talking to others, he became a machine. A mechanism only doing what he's told. Not thinking, only being. He was unsure how many days they had been on the road, nor did he care.

When the century finally arrived to reinforce the men that were already embroiled in battle, there was no time to set up camp or prepare. In uncharacteristic fashion, Kornelius's century dropped all unnecessary equipment and charged to the front of the battlefield. They had prepared for this day and were almost relieved that it had finally come.

The Celts were shockingly large. Kornelius had heard about their physique but was still surprised to actually see it. He quickly assessed his adversary's fighting style, withdrew his *gladius,* and began sparring. While the Celts were physically larger, they fought with abandon and emotion. The Romans had been trained to fight with structure and strategy. Kornelius easily killed one Celt after another, using his smaller, more flexible body to outwit his large opponents. Once the battle had been won, the men walked through the sea of Celt bodies, stabbing them to insure death. They also pulled off jewelry and other valuables they could find on the remains.

As they did this, Kornelius, Atticus, and Britannicus discussed their first battle.

"Was it like you thought it would be?" Atticus asked no one in particular.

"It was easier than I thought. There was really no challenge at all, even though they were much bigger and more savage," Britannicus responded calmly while pulling his *gladius* out of a Celt's chest.

"I thought it would bother me to kill another person, but after Julius, I don't think killing will mean anything to me one way or the other," Atticus said flatly.

Kornelius felt more alive than ever. It was strange to him that the way out of the mental stupor he had experienced was to take the lives of others. He did not want to convey that thought, however. "We were prepared and protecting ourselves. I should think it was an ordinary day for a Roman soldier."

Britannicus rolled his eyes. "You might as well be a brick wall, Kornelius. By the gods, you could bore the enemy to death. Here, give me your *gladius*. Simply talk and you'll kill them," he said, lunging for Kornelius' sword.

Kornelius anticipated the movement and shifted enough to the side to cause Britannicus to lose his mark and subsequently his balance. He tumbled onto a dead Celt. Kornelius's dimples escaped when he smirked at his comrade and said, "Perhaps you should consider becoming more like a brick wall." He turned away and continued stabbing bodies as he headed toward his abandoned equipment.

Chapter 17

That evening, as they ate their simple meal, Atticus sat next to Kornelius. "You must get along better with Britannicus. You're endangering the entire unit with your arguing."

"*Our* arguing? It's completely him. I simply strive to keep him in his place. Why don't you talk to him about your concern?"

"You are both children, even now. Mark me. This behavior will get us all killed, either by the enemy or by the centurion. It keeps us all distracted. Today, for example. What if one of those Celts was still alive? One of us could have been stabbed during your disagreement," Atticus said with sincere concern in his voice.

"You are overreacting. Besides, I cannot think of a more honorable death than to be killed defending Rome," Kornelius retorted.

"I'm glad you've made our death your decision, Kornelius. And technically it won't be because we're defending Rome. It will be because you cannot work within your unit." Atticus abruptly got up and entered the tent for the night.

Kornelius sat up for a while longer. He didn't feel like sleeping just yet and offered to take the first watch so that he could sort out what Atticus had said.

Chapter 18

Scouts returned one evening to report that a new wave of Celts was marching toward them. The unit, like all the others, quickly pulled up camp and gathered to hear the plans for the impending battle. Once again, Kornelius went from mental oblivion to anticipation and excitement. As the century marched onward, there was a spring in Kornelius's step. His heart began racing, and he felt alive.

The century split in different directions as they prepared to meet the Celts in their own battle-created theatre. That night, they deviated from their usual camp preparation and instead slept by unit at the perimeter. Each unit was responsible for the safety of their tent. The watch shifts were shorter so that each man would have a reasonable amount of sleep before the anticipated battle the next morning.

Kornelius could not sleep. He looked forward to the battle and could not stop thinking about how it would feel to have his *gladius* penetrate his opponent's chest. His nostrils flared as he imagined the eyes of his dying victim, looking at him first with hatred, then fear, and then death.

At last, morning came and it was time to prepare. Kornelius was the first one up, nudging the others to make ready. Brittanicus was lying still, pretending to sleep, when Kornelius placed his foot under his back and lifted it up. As he did this, Brittanicus grabbed his foot and quickly thrust it upward, causing Kornelius to fall on his *gluteus maximus*. The others in the unit laughed at Kornelius, except for Atticus, who looked on in horror.

Their unit was positioned on the side of the theatre and would be the closest to the incoming Celts. They were to conceal themselves and then flank the enemy once the majority had entered into battle, taking out as many as possible before being discovered. There were other units with similar orders positioned strategically. The unit hid their equipment and made ready. They could hear the drums of the Celts and see the plume of dust as they descended into the theatre. The Romans had the element of surprise and the luxury of determining where the battle would take place. They waited like spiders whose web had just been spun.

As the Celts entered the area, the front units began to shoot arrows and javelins. The Celts did not hesitate but instead yelled gutturally as they charged the Romans. More and more Celts came rushing in, axes in hand, flinging themselves and their weapons about in reckless abandon. The ferocity of this enemy was unlike anything the Romans had encountered. They behaved like rabid dogs as they approached, which aided the Romans in surprising them from behind.

The signal came for the flanking units to move, and with stealthy speed the units were able to completely surround the Celts in minutes. Not having the full load of equipment hanging from their bodies was a freeing elixir to the burdened Romans, who had traveled so far on foot.

The unit quickly began felling the Celts at the back, stepping over bodies to move toward the front of the battle. Kornelius's heart pounded as he pushed and pulled his *gladius* out of his opponents' chests and backs. There was no other feeling like it. The way the *gladius* entered the skin, the sound of it meeting with flesh and bone, the power that surged through his body as he ended the lives of his opponents.

Within minutes, the Roman Army had overtaken the Celts. It had been too easy and a bit disappointing for the men who had been so highly trained for combat. Was there not an army in all the world that could challenge them?

Atticus and Britannicus were beside Kornelius as they reached the front line of the army. As was customary, they killed most of the Celts, saving some to be used as slaves. As the last of the enemy were being killed, Kornelius lifted his *gladius* for a final strike. His opponent had fought hard but simply did not have the flexibility to gain an advantage. As he lifted his sword, Brittanicus rushed in, pushing Kornelius out of the way in order to make the kill himself. Kornelius, shocked to be on the ground himself, lunged up with arms spread. When his body connected with Brittanicus, he wrapped his arms around him and squeezed. The momentum of the lunge knocked both men on the ground. The Celt, still alive, took advantage of the situation and rolled to the side, stabbing first Kornelius and then Britannicus. Atticus rushed in to help, but was too late. The Celt was now once again in full battle mode and flung his sword at Atticus, hitting his chest in a mortal deathblow.

Others from their unit were able to kill the Celt. Brittannicus and Atticus were dead. Kornelius's wound was superficial and would heal. He was carried off to the camp for medicine and wrappings.

As he recovered, General Scipio visited him. "Kornelius, you have been an excellent warrior. Many have noticed your fighting ability and strategy. As soon as you've recovered, I am going to promote you to be my aide. I will need someone to replace me, as I am getting too old to continue for much longer. I believe that you have what it takes to be that man."

"I am most honored, General, to be that man. Thank you for your faith in me," Kornelius said, happy that he had been granted such a prestigious and powerful position, yet mournful that he had lost two of his brothers in combat.

As he lay in recovery, Kornelius realized that Atticus had been correct all along. He would have to rise above his feelings and learn to suppress them if he and his soon-to-be men were to survive.

Bridge

"Why do I not remember from one lesson to the next?"

"You do remember each lesson. You are not allowed to begin a new one until you're satisfied that you've learned the last one."

"I meant, why do I not remember my previous experiences when I am in a new lesson?"

"Because that would distract you from focusing on the lesson at hand."

"So if I remembered Amayah from my second lesson, or I remembered Amam from my third lesson, it would distract me from the lesson at hand?"

"Correct. You would be too filled with preexisting emotions to understand the present circumstances, which you are given for educational purposes. You sense that you've known them before, but you are not consciously certain."

"Then why do you place me with the same beings each time? And why do I not interact with them here?"

"So many questions, all of which you will be prepared to answer yourself in time. Analyze what you've learned up until now. This is the path to all of the answers you seek, which are miniscule to how much more there is to know. Communicating with me at this point only delays your progress."

England

Chapter 19

Ainsley was covered in sweat. Her breath was haggard and quick. The midwife could do no more for her. Her labor had gone on for hours upon hours, and still the baby refused to crown. There was nothing more anyone could do for Ainsley. She had led a wonderful life and had given birth to a beautiful baby girl two years earlier. But now, this birth would not end well. She was going to die, and everyone in the household knew it. The family gathered around to say their farewells, to hold her hand, to kiss her forehead. What would the family do without her? She was the glue that held everyone together. She was the unspoken leader of the family, even though she was a woman.

With her emerald green eyes filled with tears, she gave her last breath. The midwife took out a knife and gently cut the baby out of the womb. He was weak and exhausted. He needed nourishment, or he too would die. The baby suckled his dead mother's breast as the family searched for a suitable food substitute for him.

Chapter 20

As Keaton grew, it became apparent that he had a gift for art. His father was gone most of the time, and he and his sister, Jayne, were often left alone. To pass the time, he had begun drawing, first with coal that had cooled from the fireplace and then with paint that was given to him when his father realized his talent. He liked drawing pictures of his family members, especially Jayne, who had a bright red face and happy disposition.

When it was time to begin school, Keaton and Jayne walked together to the schoolhouse each day, often playing games along the way. Keaton's talent continued to improve, and by the end of his schooling it was clear that he would become a portraitist.

His father set him up in a small studio in central London. Keaton placed completed portraits in the studio's windows so that people could see and appreciate his work. Soon, his talent became popular for its originality and flair. One day, a man came in and asked if he would create a portrait of his daughter. Keaton agreed to come to their home the following day.

A maid opened the door when he knocked and lead him to the parlor. As he walked in, the air left his lungs and his heart began to pound. There, sitting before him, was the most beautiful woman he had ever seen. Her mere presence caused an unfamiliar stirring within him. He did not know exactly how he felt; he was only aware that this woman undid him and left him vulnerable and emotionally naked. He struggled to compose himself and finally was able to say, "You must be Batilda." His voice faught to remain calm and rational.

She pursed her lips, revealing a slight cleft in her chin. "I am. And you must be Keaton. I'm pleased to meet you," she said as she walked toward him with her hand out.

Keaton took her hand and bowed. As their hands touched, the unexplained internal battle within him raged even more. He was perplexed at what was going on within him, both mentally and physically. *Is this love or hate?* he asked himself, not having the slightest clue what the answer was. "Shall we begin?" he managed to blurt out.

Sheer will forced his hand to begin painting Batilda's portrait. Her beauty was stunning. She had dark auburn hair and thick red lips accentuated by pale, nearly translucent skin. Her eyes had a fire in them and indicated intellect coupled with a feistiness that could mean trouble. Keaton decided that he needed more time with her in order to sort out his feelings. Toward the end of the session he announced that he would need to come back at least a few more times in order to truly capture her essence. Batilda seemed amused by this, as if she knew that it was simply a ruse to see more of her. Keaton was sure that someone of her stature and beauty probably had many men interested in her, and his actions were probably expected. If he had not been interested, he concluded, then she would have been surprised.

On his way back to the studio, Keaton contemplated what had happened. He was unable to work anymore and simply closed his studio for the day.

As he continued to frequent Batilda's home, he became more accustomed to his involuntary feelings in her presence. They were not receding, but at least he could better conceal them now. In time, the portrait was complete. He stood back and looked at his work. It was by far the best he had ever painted. He was pleased. He invited Batilda to look at it.

She walked slowly toward the portrait, looking into his eyes as she walked. Only when she stopped in front of the painting did she steal her eyes away from him and look. She gasped.

"Oh, Keaton! It's perfect. It's as if I'm looking into a mirror. Thank you!" She turned to kiss him on the cheek.

Keaton's stoic charade could not withstand the kiss. He shuttered at the sensation of her lips on his face. Once again, he was undone. "It was easy with such a lovely subject," he managed to push out of his mouth.

"It's a shame you're done," she said flirtatiously. "I'll miss seeing those dimples each day." She ran her finger along his cheek.

Keaton struggled to maintain composure as he said, "Batilda, would you like to have tea with me?" His heart leapt for joy when she agreed. He could not believe his good fortune that such a fine lady would agree to spend time with him.

The two were married a year later. Keaton's reputation spread, and soon he moved his studio to a better part of town to show his value to the aristocrats of London. The couple moved into a large home where many a child was conceived and born.

Life was happy for Keaton and Batilda. Their rather large family experienced few problems.

One day Keaton was summoned to go to Westminster Abbey to create a portrait of the Archbishop. He had never been inside the church and was surprised at its grandeur. As he began, the Archbishop asked him if he was familiar with Christianity. Keaton replied that he was not. Since the two would be together for some time, he asked the Archbishop to explain the religion to him.

"Several hundred years ago," the Archbishop began, "there was a man called Jesus …" The conversation went on to explain how he had died for everyone's sins, and the concept of forgiveness.

The more Keaton heard, the more interested he became. Religion was completely unfamiliar to him. He enjoyed talking to his subjects as he created their portraits, and as a result he learned about many, many things. Christianity was by far the most fascinating topic he had encountered.

He broached the subject with Batilda one evening. She was far less interested in the topic than Keaton was or had been. However, she grudgingly agreed to attend church one Sunday to appease her husband. Keaton found the experience to be exhilarating. It excited him greatly, and he was amazed that such a wondrous way to view the world had never been discussed in his presence before. He became thirsty for more knowledge about the church and its Bible. He insisted that his family attend services each Sunday, taking Jayne and her family to join them. He discussed what he was learning with his subjects, which interested some and very much disinterested others.

While working on a portrait of a monk several months later, word was sent from home that one of his children, Sutton, had died. He ran all the way home, the monk following closely behind. When they arrived, the rest of the family had already gathered around the dead child. Batlilda bolted up to Keaton, throwing the small boy's toy at him, asking, "This is what your God does for you?" She collapsed and wept. Keaton ignored her and slowly walked up to the child.

Everything was in slow motion; he couldn't believe what he was seeing. He kept thinking his son would open his piercing blue eyes, get up any second, and run off to play. As the realization began to sink in, Keaton walked slowly into his study, closed the door, and locked it.

Keaton's perfect world, the one where he was successful and sought-after, where he had a beautiful wife and children, came collapsing down around him. Only in his excruciating grief did he come to realize that nothing was permanent. Instead of being stationary, life was like a river that moved sometimes slow and sometimes fast, sometimes smoothly and sometimes over rocks. There was a knock on the door.

"Not now," Keaton said, wanting to continue his line of thought uninterrupted.

"Sir, I think I may be of help," responded the monk, who had followed him home.

"You cannot. Please leave," Keaton said, irritated that this man was pulling him out of his own thoughts.

There were more knocks on the door, followed by another plea to let him in. Keaton, now unable to think alone for the moment, sighed and opened the door. He turned and walked back into the study, flopping in an overstuffed wingback chair without so much as looking at the monk. The monk walked in and closed the door, locking it.

"Sutton is in heaven," the monk began. "The Lord decided he wanted to take him home now." He had often said these words to those who had lost a loved one.

"Why would the Lord need someone so young, monk? Tell me that," Keaton growled.

"We do not profess to know why things happen as they do. We just know that our Lord is loving and forgiving and that he does what he does for reasons that we don't always understand."

"That sounds more like something you've been taught, rather than something you actually believe yourself," scoffed Keaton.

"I have been taught these words, and I do believe them. It is your understandable grief that causes you to not also fall back on your lessons. In all that is happening to you and your family right now, it is very important that you remember that Sutton is in a better place." The monk touched Keaton's chest, over his heart, and continued, "You know this to be true. Hold onto that knowledge, and let it provide you with comfort and courage."

Keaton reached over to the nearby desk and grabbed an ink blotter, throwing it across the room in one motion. "I know nothing right now except that my beloved child is in the other room, dead. Leave now."

The monk made the sign of the cross and left, closing the door behind him. As he walked down the hallway, he could hear the door lock behind him.

Alone once more, Keaton attempted to reconstruct his string of thoughts. The river. Yes. Lots of different rivers, some of them occasionally intersecting, some going straight out to sea. So many different paths, each one altered by a slight change in course. A change of course could be intentional or unintentional, created by one's own hand or someone else's. Where did God fit into this? Or did he? Was there a god who managed the rivers, or were they simply left to chance? Was God created through the minds of men in order to help comfort and make sense of life?

He spent many days pondering these questions. He busied himself with more portrait sittings to suppress his grief. During the sittings, he asked clients their thoughts on the subject of life and God. There were many varying opinions, which only served to stir Keaton's desire for the truth.

Months later, he was creating a portrait of an elderly man and began asking him the questions he had asked so many times before. The man smiled kindly, as an adult would when a child asks a simple question.

"You want to know if there is a God, and if not, is there a meaning for our lives?" the man said rhetorically. "What a strange subject to bring up under these circumstances. Let me ask you, do you feel there is a God?"

"I did. I was quite convinced of it from the moment I learned about Jesus. But then my son died, and I couldn't imagine a god who would take my son away at such a young age. Now, I just want the truth," Keaton said a bit sadly as he continued painting.

"So when life was going well for you, you believed in the creator. When something tragic happened, you stopped believing. Your logic states that nothing bad happens to Christians."

"Yes, I suppose it does—if Christianity is real, that is," Keaton said slowly, adding, "But that's the crux of it, don't you see? How do you know?"

"Indeed, how do you know?" the man responded. There was silence as Keaton painted. Finally the man continued, "Let's follow the path of no god and see how far it takes us. If there was no god, then how did we get where we are today? How did we separate ourselves so decisively from the rest of the creatures?"

"I haven't the foggiest, and I don't see how that proves anything one way or the other. Just because we don't know something doesn't mean it's by God's hand."

"But we don't know if it is *not* by God's hand. You see, the point of faith is that you believe in something without having solid evidence. You felt it in your heart. Indeed, you were zealous. Perhaps the death of your son was a test. You believed that there was a heaven, and now, if you still believed that, you would have a peacefulness knowing that you'll see him again one day and that he is in a good place now."

"You've given me more to think about. Thank you," Keaton said sincerely. He did not want to continue this line of conversation. He just wanted to be left alone with his thoughts.

As time went on, the sorrow of losing Sutton subsided. He continued his thirst for the truth and interviewed hundreds of people on the subject of spirituality. As he grew old, he asked a colleague to create a portrait of himself so that his children would remember him when he was gone.

During the sitting, he asked the painter his opinion on religion. The painter smiled and said, "Yes, I've heard that you often ask about such things. I don't have any answer for you, Keaton. But tell me, what have you learned in all this time, conversing with so many on the subject?"

Keaton smiled. He hadn't thought about what others may say about him, but of course it made sense that he would have a reputation for being inquisitive on this particular subject. He looked up at the ceiling, composing his answer. No one had asked him his own thoughts in a very long time, and he hadn't really considered a specific opinion for himself. He had always been more interested in compiling the beliefs of others instead.

"I cannot say exactly that I have found the answer. What I can tell you is that people have varying thoughts on religion. Even those who agree in principle that there is a creator will have different opinions on the details of the creator. If people believe because it fits into their lifestyle, or if they live their lifestyle because they believe, I am not sure. But I will say that most of the people who have religion struggle more to live clean lives. I wouldn't say that they are purer, or more peaceful, but that they might try harder to do the right thing. Of course, there are exceptions, but that appears to be the overall case."

"Interesting observation. But I must ask, what do you believe now?"

"I believe there must be a creator. I feel in my heart that it is the only thing that makes sense for this world. I cannot prove it. But when I let go of myself and let Him guide me, I feel more grounded and at peace. After all this time and all of the discussions, that is the essence of everything to me. It's what I come back to any time my mind tries to apply intellect to any other theory."

Bridge

"There are many before me and many behind me. I found that I could tell the difference this time rather easily."

"Yes, that is the natural progression."

"Why wasn't Amayah in this life with me?"

"I'm intrigued that you continue to inquire about Amayah. Your lives touched briefly. In this life, she was your mother, Ainsley, who passed giving birth to you. That being has moved on now. You will not encounter that one again in your lessons."

"Is there a creator?"

"You have already discovered the answer."

"What more is there for me to learn?"

"A few more things are yours to discover and experience. I will leave you now to reflect."

America

Chapter 21

Kanti's tribe, while nomadic in nature, did not move past the Great River. The chief had not allowed it. Since the beginning, it had been prohibited because the Great Spirit had said there was evil beyond. Those who dared cross were not seen again, creating a certainty among the tribe that the Great Spirit had shown them mercy by informing them of such perils.

But Kanti's heart felt drawn to go beyond. She was a woman and therefore not allowed to even hunt with the men. Her brother, Bedagi, secretly allowed her to hunt with him. She would pretend to be out picking berries, or washing in the Great River. Bedagi knew her better than anyone and felt that if the Great Spirit had placed the desire to hunt in Kanti's heart that it should be. She was good at it, too. Her bow and arrow were surer than anyone's in the tribe. The glow in her checks and the way her dimples slowly revealed themselves when she found her mark only strengthened Bedagi's resolve that this was the right thing to do. But there was great risk if they were ever discovered. To overstep the tribe's law would result in severe punishment for them both.

As they were out hunting one day, Kanti tracked her prey. She was so focused that she did not realize that she was being tracked as well. As she readied her bow and arrow, a large hand clasped her face while another wrapped around her waist, squeezing the air from her lungs. She was rendered immediately helpless. There were many twinkles of light before she slipped into unconsciousness.

She awoke to find herself surrounded by men with white faces. They smelled horribly and talked in a language that she did not understand. They had belongings that she did not recognize. After she assessed her immediate surroundings, she began to look past the campsite. The terrain was unfamiliar to her. Slowly, horror began to creep into her blood, causing her heart to pump rapidly. One of the men was talking to her, but she could not understand what he was saying. All she could do was look back at him with wide eyes. He spoke louder, as if this would help her to understand his words, but it did not help. In fact, it frightened her more.

Another man came up to her with a more soothing voice and handed her a strange item. It was like her wooden bowl, but it had been flattened. It was not made of wood, but of something else, something gray and cold to the touch. The food on top smelled strange, but good. She realized that she was hungry and took the flattened bowl in one hand and reached for the food with the other. The nicer of the men gently pulled away the hand she was about to use to feed herself and placed in it a strange item that was like a stick, but made of the same grayish material. It was much sturdier than a stick. The man motioned to her how to use it. He said "Fork" as he mimicked how she should be eating. Then, he pointed to the flattened bowl and said, "Plate." She tried to say both of these words, but they sounded so odd, the men laughed at her. All except for the nice one. The one with the golden hair and kind smile. He ignored the others and repeated the words over and over until she could repeat them accurately.

Kanti did not understand why she was here with these men or what they had planned for her. She had never been away from her tribe, and they had not encountered any violence with other tribes. She was completely at a loss for what might be in store for her. She hoped that they would eventually take her back where she belonged.

As time went on, she learned how to speak the language. Once she was able to communicate she understood that the white men had taken her for a threat. They had been out hunting themselves and feared that she would see them and alert her tribe, and that they would attack to defend their land.

Kanti, while she now understood what had happened, did not understand "defending their land." The land did not belong to people. It was simply part of the Great Spirit's way of providing sustenance to all who lived. Until the day she died, Kanti did not understand the concept of property ownership.

She was a young girl when they took her, and they debated what to do with her once the danger of being discovered was no more. Some wanted to release her; others wanted to keep her as a sort of slave to do the cooking, cleaning, and other work that they did not particularly like doing themselves. But once they saw her ability to hunt, all debate dissolved, and she became one of them. This was her new tribe.

While she was terrified at first, Kanti soon became happier with these white-faced men than she had been before. They were nomadic and in fact had crossed the Great River several times back and forth. There was no evil there. They hunted, eating the meat and trading the pelts for supplies. She was allowed to hunt with them, being at least as good as they were. They treated her as one of them, all except the man who had been the first to be kind to her. He looked at her differently than the others. His name was Seth, and when he did look at her, her heart beat faster and her cheeks burned.

She had given up her tribe's attire and now wore the same clothing as the men. If not for her petite frame and long dark hair, one would have thought she was a man herself.

Chapter 22

One day, the group was in a small town, trading their pelts. Several men strutted around as if they were very important. They all wore the exact same clothing. Kanti thought they were funny, the way they walked and how they took themselves so seriously. She stifled a laugh as one pranced by. He stopped, turned, and looked at her with rage in his eyes. Her dimpled smile vanished as he raised his hand and punched her in the cheek. She fell backward, not anticipating the blow, and hit the back of her head on the wooden porch of the trading post. Blood began to ooze from the wound. Seth pulled his weapon from his belt and killed the soldier.

They knew they would not have much time before the rest of the soldiers discovered what Seth had done. The other men took the dead solider and hid him under horse blankets. Seth scooped up the dazed Kanti and followed closely behind. They quickly headed for the nearby mountains, knowing they would be harder to track up there.

For several days they continued through the rough terrain. They were unsure if anyone knew what they had done or if they were being tracked. They were not going to take any chances. As they journeyed through the mountain range, Seth grabbed Kanti's hand and pulled her back so that the rest of the men were well in front of them and out of hearing range.

She stopped, questioning him with her eyes. He held both of her hands and softly said, "I knew I loved you when I saw you laying on the ground, bleeding. I realized I never want to lose you, Kanti. Please do me the honor of becoming my wife." Kanti had not expected this and gasped. Seth's face filled with despair, and he turned and began walking toward the men. "I'm sorry," he said over his shoulder. "I was just joking."

Kanti stood there momentarily, soaking in what had happened. Then, she raced with all of her speed to catch up to Seth. Now it was her turn to grab his hand. She pulled too hard, whipping him around to her. She gasped again to see tears in his piercing blue eyes. She flung her arms around him and whispered in his ear, "Yes."

The two exchanged vows, for they were in the wilderness and marriage formalities were not available this far from civilization. They continued with the other men until Kanti became thick with child. She had to stop hiking and hunting for the time being. Seth told the others to go without them, and that they would meet up with them in time, if they could. Now they were alone. Seth found a cave at the base of one of the mountains within a crevice. He killed the bears that were living there, cleaned it out, and used the bearskins as bedding for Kanti and the child that would soon be in their arms. Winter would come soon. Seth hunted farther and farther away from the cave to make sure he had enough to last them when they became snowed in.

While they had spent many winter seasons in harsh conditions, he was unsure of how Kanti and the child would do after the birth. Neither of them knew much about childbirth. Kanti had watched as the women in the tribe would help one another, but she had never participated in the process.

Seth was a few miles from the cave when the first snowstorm hit. It started as a heavy rain, then turned to ice and then snow. It was coming down heavily and sideways. Seth could hardly see in front of him. He quickly headed back to the cave, hoping that his inner compass was correct. He could not use visual cues in this weather and feared he did not have much time before he would not be able to travel at all. Despite his determination, he had to seek shelter or he would perish. He quickly found a base of a large rock and began digging underneath it. He would make a small habitat to wait out the storm. Hopefully it would not last too long.

***

While Seth sought shelter, Kanti was feeling sharp pains. She knew the time was coming and that she may have to give birth alone. She crawled on her hands and knees to the far corner of the cave, dragging one of the rugs with her. She had built a large fire toward the front of the cave to keep the area warm, understanding that she may not be able to tend to it later. She propped her back against the wall and closed her eyes as the pain increased and came more frequently.

Kanti was covered in sweat and panting. Her legs were spread, and she could feel the crown of the baby's head between her legs. She groaned as she pushed and pushed until the baby was completely out. It was a boy, and he seemed furious that he had been plucked from his nice bed. She laughed at his fury as he opened his mouth and she could see the back of his throat.

"Oh you are mighty, little one!" Kanti said proudly. "Wait until your papa sees you!" As she said this, more pain pierced through her. It caught her off guard, and she nearly dropped the baby in her arms. She braced herself as the pain coursed through her body again and again. Then, she felt another crown between her legs. She panted until she could hardly breathe at all. She had placed her firstborn beside her so that she could help bring this one out with both of her hands. It did not come as easily. She had to push more and harder to bring the body out even a little bit. She saw twinkling lights in front of her eyes, and then she saw nothing at all.

***

When Seth returned to their cave, he found Kanti unconscious and two babies, one beside her and one between her legs. His heart raced as he tried to determine what he should do first. He reached for Kanti's hand. It was warm; a good sign. He gently laid it back down and then picked up the baby between her legs. The eyes immediately opened, and Seth's heart swelled. It was the most beautiful baby girl he had ever seen. Even being just born, he could tell that she had wisdom in those little eyes and the beautiful turned-up nose. He gently laid her down and picked up the baby beside Kanti. Unlike his sister, he kept his eyes closed but cried the most urgent and outraged cry Seth had ever heard. "Oh you will be a hunter, as soon as you learn how to channel that energy!" he said with joy.

Then, his thoughts went back to Kanti. She was breathing but still asleep. He placed the babies on either side of her and went to fill the kettle with snow. He placed it over the fire until it became warm and then moved it to the back of the cave. His hands came from the kettle to the babies, rinsing the blood and mucus from their bodies. He cut the cords and tied them into knots, then wrapped them snugly in rabbit pelts and laid them back down next to their mother. All the while, the girl watched him like an owl. The boy was still screaming, but Seth could tell he was becoming weaker. He dipped his hand in the water once more and began smoothing Kanti's face and pulling her hair back. He realized how exhausted she must be, but she would have to feed the babies soon. He kept placing warm water on her face, legs, arms, and hands until she slowly came into consciousness.

Upon seeing Seth, she slowly smiled and said, "Hello, Papa." Seth kissed her forehead and replied, "Hello, Mama." She looked into his eyes for a brief, contented moment and then, as if she just remembered, snapped her head toward her babies. Seth smiled sweetly and said, "They're both fine, but I think they're hungry. I can't help you with that."

She hoisted herself up to a sitting position and whispered, "Help me. I'm not sure how to do this."

Seth picked up the boy, since the cave would be more peaceful once his cries were stifled. The baby attacked Kanti's breast with such fervor that she yelped in pain and surprise. "He seems to know exactly what he's supposed to do. At least one of us does," she said playfully. She reached out her arm for the baby girl, who was now watching her mother intently—that is, until her mouth found her mother's warm milk.

"We will call her Pavati," Kanti said. "In my first language, it means 'from the clear waters.'"

The family stayed in the cave until the children were able to walk. They went hunting together and prepared their meals together. Everyone had daily responsibilities. Eventually, they set out to hunt for pelts and follow the trails that led to trading posts. Kanti and Seth preferred a life of wandering and seeing new things, and they continued to live this way until they were too old to do otherwise.

Bridge

"Oh, that was amazing. Existing as a female is quite different."

"Yes. And very important to your readiness."

"I feel like Atlantis was a distant dream. Did it even happen?"

"Yes. Everything that has crossed before you, even dreams, has a purpose."

"I must be very close now—though I still do not know what exactly I'm close to."

"It is true that you are close, but there are still things you must learn. Think now and ponder what you've been shown."

Africa

Chapter 23

Kadeem ran across the plain as fast as he could, stopping now and then to catch his breath under a rock or foliage. A large snake had nearly made a meal out of him. He had been sunning himself and had nearly fallen asleep when the snake was about to bite him. As luck would have it, a small piece of gravel had shifted just in time to alert Kadeem to his impending doom. He bolted. No snake was as fast as him. In fact, most of the other lizards weren't as fast as Kadeem either.

He usually enjoyed running and could go for hours without resting, but now he needed to make sure he was far away from the snake before slowing down. This was not a joy run. This was survival. Snakes could be so quiet. He had lost many friends to those vile creatures.

At last, he felt he was far enough away from danger to rest. He found a rock that he could blend in nicely with. He selected a spot where the sunlight would envelope him for most of the remainder of the day. He was a bit hungry, but he would wait until dusk to find some delicious ants for his supper. He settled in and dozed off on the warm rock.

Toward dusk, he began to feel slightly cooler and instinctively knew it was time to prepare for night. He opened his eyes and looked around. He stretched his four legs by doing push-ups while looking around for a colony that would suffice for his dinner. When he turned to look behind, he noticed his friend with the funny freckles, Laik, was beginning to wake up as well. It bothered Kadeem slightly that he hadn't heard Laik join him on the rock. First the snake and now Laik. He must be slipping. He would have to be more careful.

"Do you want to catch dinner with me?" Kadeem asked.

"Just thinking the same thing, my friend. That colony over there?" Laik responded.

"Yes, exactly. We'll have to move fast before they retreat. You take that side, and I'll take the other. On your mark. Get set. Go!" Kadeem said as he leapt effortlessly toward the mound. Laik was just slightly behind his long tail.

It was pleasant having ants for a change. Usually, Kadeem had worms or roaches. While ants were smaller, they had a distinctive taste that made up for the fact that he had to catch more of them to fill his belly. It was a great way to end his busy day. He said good night to Laik and found a perfectly sized cavern to rest in for the remainder of the night.

As the sun came up, Kadeem found a worm for his breakfast, then did his push-ups, found a good rock, and sunned himself. He would go for a long run later, as soon as he had warmed up. With his belly full and his morning routine complete, Kadeem closed his eyes and enjoyed the sunlight. Just as he dozed, a snake slithered silently toward the back of the rock. It opened its mouth as it hurled itself toward Kadeem's body. It would have to reach the body because the lizard's tail would easily break off, and his prey would escape him once more.

This time, he was successful. No gravel to compromise his position too early. Kadeem made a tasty morning meal.

Bridge

"I didn't anticipate that!"

"No one does. It's a surprise, but one of the most important lessons you will learn."

"Yes, I see that it is important. I understand nature completely now, I think. The purity of it."

"You are very close. But it is not just nature that you are learning. It is balance as well. There is complication and simplicity. Light and darkness. Movement and stillness. The balance of existence can be replayed throughout the entire spectrum. It is the single most important thing that you must understand. Balance."

Germany

Chapter 24

The work was long and difficult. Konrad and his family had been farming for generations and did not know any different. Located in the German heartland, their land had nearly always yielded abundantly, and therefore not many family members felt the need to leave. Their lives were simple and well defined. Births, deaths, and even marriages usually took place within the family's expansive compound. Only occasionally did they leave, and then only to sell crops or purchase needed items. Konrad loved going to town with his father. He would do extra chores so that he could be missed for the entire day that it took to get there and back.

As they pulled into the store, a stout woman in a fine dress marched up to his father. "Sir, does this child attend school?" she demanded undiplomatically.

"He is taught by his family what he needs to know," Konrad's father responded, placing his hand on his son's shoulder.

The woman pulled out a clipboard and began flipping sheets of paper over the top, sliding her index finger down the next sheet and then flipping it over. Konrad wasn't sure what was happening, but he sensed that it wasn't good. His father stood still, not taking his hand off of his son's shoulder and not saying a word.

"His name is not on my list. I'm afraid he must start attending school. It's the law." The way the word "law" languished on her thick tongue made Konrad angry, although he didn't know why. "You see, we can no longer depend on farming families to properly educate our young people. There is just too much to learn, and I'm afraid farmers have been very much sheltered from all of the new technology that abounds now. The government had no choice but to step in and help these poor children. They'll never grow up properly if we allow them to continue without a proper education."

Konrad's father's voice turned icy. "My son is being taught everything he needs to know to be a good farmer and a good man. The government does not know what is best for him. I do." Now the son was terrified, having never heard that chilling tone before.

"Say what you will. I am putting his name on my list. Unfortunately, there are no schools nearby yet, so we will have to place him at a residential school in Munich. I will send for him a week from today. Be sure he is packed and ready to go. The government will supply him with what he needs." She stalked off, not waiting for a reply. She was carrying her clipboard and looking to the left and right as she proceeded down the main street.

Konrad's father quickly finished their business and began asking those in the small town about this woman and her demands. Apparently, it had all been true. She had been in the area for about a week, preparing to herd all of the school-aged children off to Munich to be educated. Konrad's family farm had been so remote that word hadn't got to them in time to hide Konrad. Now he was on their list, and there was little they could do about it other than comply or have their land taken from them.

Konrad waited at the edge of his property with his mother and father. The rest of the family had kept away, not wanting any more of the children to be identified and carted off. His father had his hand on his shoulder again, and Konrad could feel a slight trembling from his father. It was at that moment that Konrad fully understood that his family was not in control of their own destiny. He realized that things had changed, and now something called "the government" had taken control away from them. He would remember this epiphany for the remainder of his life.

The cart rolled up. In it were several other children, boys and girls, all looking as terrified and angry as Konrad felt.

They journeyed all day and into the night. Most of the children had fallen asleep along the way, leaning on each other for comfort. The steady sound of the cart lulled their tired little bodies to sleep after what had been a very stressful day.

Konrad's eyes opened quickly when they finally stopped at a large building in the biggest city he had ever seen. Most of the children were wide awake now. It was still dark, but he felt that perhaps the sun would begin rising soon. Farmers' children knew how to tell time without watches or clocks.

They were instructed to take all of their belongings into the foyer. As they walked in, a tall slender woman stood waiting for them, clipboard in hand. She did not smile and in fact looked rather mean as she read off the names of the children, expecting them to acknowledge when they heard theirs. Her hair was pulled back so tightly that it almost made her eyes also pull back. Konrad knew this woman would be trouble and resolved to steer clear of her whenever possible.

He shared a room with two other boys: Peer, who had a funny turned-up nose, and Larenzo, who had freckles on his cheeks. Thankfully, the three became best friends. After a brief time of trial and error, they determined how to stay out of trouble and yet sneak out for fun when no one was looking.

Konrad not only got used to the school, but life in the city as well. As much as he had been angry that the government took him away from his previous life and his family, he knew that he would not go back there. In fact, learning here was very easy for him. He was smarter and more advanced than the other students. The headmistress continued to pull him up grade after grade because he was learning so quickly. She secretly knew the three boys were sneaking out but let them go because they were doing so well in their studies, although the other two were not nearly as naturally intelligent as Konrad.

Chapter 25

Soon, Konrad became bored with school and with Munich. Both were now too small for him. He craved more knowledge and a bigger city. He went in to talk to the headmistress, whose hair was still pulled back too tightly. He was no longer afraid of her. Now, he felt he would have a much higher station in life than her and simply needed to maneuver his way into a more satisfying situation for himself.

"I think I'm ready for college, Headmistress."

"Yes, I would agree. You've done well here, Konrad, and we have little else to teach you. Would you like to be returned to your family?" she asked, trying to sound nice, but still sounding mean. Konrad could read her intentions easily now.

"No, thank you. I want to go to college."

"Ah. Excellent choice, Konrad. Excellent," she said, clasping her hands together and touching her mouth with them. "Now, let's see, there is the University of Munich, which is a very good school—"

Konrad interrupted her. "I want to go to a university in the United States. Actually, New York, to be specific." He knew she would not only be shocked, but also provide several reasons why he could not go. He waited patiently for her to respond predictably.

With her brow furrowed, she shook her head. "You are too young, Konrad. You have no money, and you do not know how to properly take care of yourself. It is an impossible dream you have."

"I see, Headmistress. I did not think you would help me, but out of respect, I decided to ask you anyway. Thank you for your time." Konrad smiled with his infectious dimples and strolled out of the office, turning to close the double doors with both hands.

Once his view of her was concealed by the doors, he ran to his room and began packing his things. He used the same bag that had held his farm clothes when he had first come here. Pity they did not fit anymore. He only had his school uniforms, which would be a problem. He hid the bag under his bed and opened the window. He looked both ways to make sure no one was watching and then dashed off the school grounds and into the streets of Munich. He didn't have much time. He half-trotted up one street after another until he found regular clothing, about his size, hanging out to dry on a clothesline. With no one watching, he grabbed pants and two shirts and sprinted back to the school and into his room. He rolled the clothes up and placed them in the hidden bag. Then, grabbing his books, he dashed to his classroom for his next lesson.

That night, when everyone was sleeping, including his roommates, he silently opened the window and picked up his bag, now a bit heavier with apples and cakes, and climbed out one last time. He slowly closed the window so that the night air would not wake his friends up too early. He needed all the time he could get to make his escape. He had changed into his new clothes; they were still damp, chilling him. He had studied maps and knew he had to get to the North Sea, where he would work on a ship sailing for New York.

It took more time than he thought, but nearly a year later, he set foot on the land containing the largest city in the world.

He had learned that there was no possible way to stop him from getting what he wanted. There had been many obstacles that others would deem insurmountable, yet he had been able to overcome everything that had come his way. Over the past year, he had grown to look old enough to be on his own. He no longer had to worry about somehow being caught and sent back to Germany. He had learned English. He had practiced with the Americans until his

German accent was completely gone. He had talked to them incessantly about America—the culture, the norms, the food. He felt ready to take on New York. He was invincible.

With confidence exuding from every pore, Konrad decided that he did not, in fact, need college. He was capable of teaching himself whatever he needed. Instead, he landed a job on Wall Street, where his intellect and ability to understand numbers and finance sent him up the corporate ladder quickly. At twenty, he started his own company, taking enough clients with him to turn a profit nearly immediately. He looked at the economy like a living organism. Once he understood how it drew breath, how it healed itself and grew, he easily figured out how to control it. Konrad continued to grow his company and acquire others. By the time he was twenty-five, he had amassed a fortune. But he was not satisfied.

The world, which at one point had seemed so large and exciting, now seemed very small and predictable. He longed for something challenging. The only thing left, he believed, was technology. Ironically, the German government had used ignorance of technology to pluck farm children from their families; it was how he'd ended up where he was today. Otherwise, he may never had left the farm. He could actually be plowing right now, he mused.

He considered taking a wife and having a family, yet that didn't sound interesting enough. He thought about becoming President of the United States. While he hadn't been born here, he knew people who could forge his birth and even provide a family story for him, but he felt he had more freedom not being in government. He bought two of the most technologically advanced companies in the world and began learning about all of the advancements they were secretly working on.

Despite his success and abilities, he could not find anything to satisfy him. He died a few years later. Some say he willed himself to die. There had been no other challenge for him.

Bridge

"There is nothing left for me to learn."

"I agree. You have done well."

"What happens now?"

"You go to the Beyond. You will no longer need a physical body. There is no more emotion that you will have to overcome. It is quite a different experience than anything you've encountered thus far. But you would not have been able to exist there properly without first learning what you've been taught here."

"What will be my purpose there? What do beings do there?"

"It will all make sense once you've arrived. There will be inner peace. Other beings will greet you and assist you in settling in. This is the last time that you and I will communicate. My job is to stay here and ready new beings for the Beyond. You've done well. Goodbye, Kewab."

The complete whiteness of awaiting lessons now turned to a beautiful arch of yellow, red, and a color he had not seen before. He was moving toward it, or it was moving toward him—he could not tell. Soon they would either collide or merge, and he would enter the Beyond.